NEW BOOKS FOR N

Phyllis MacAdam, *General*

Home Voices
A Sampler of Southern Writing

Mark Lucas, Editor

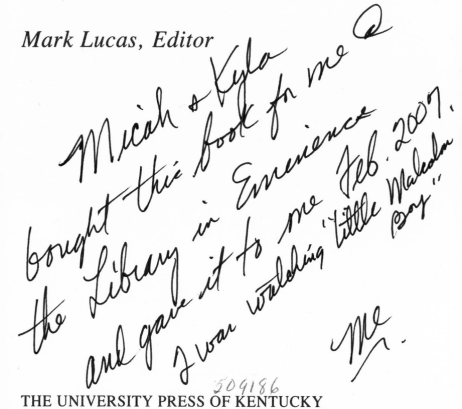

Micah + Kyla bought this book for me @ the Library in Eminence and gave it to me Feb. 2007. I was wondering "little Malcolm Boy".

me.

509186

THE UNIVERSITY PRESS OF KENTUCKY

For Mandy

This volume in the New Books for New Readers series
was supported by the Kentucky Humanities Council with
a generous grant from Financial Women International.

Copyright © 1991 by The Kentucky Humanities Council
Published by The University Press of Kentucky
Scholarly publisher for the Commonwealth,
serving Bellarmine College, Berea College, Centre
College of Kentucky, Eastern Kentucky University,
The Filson Club, Georgetown College, Kentucky
Historical Society, Kentucky State University,
Morehead State University, Murray State University,
Northern Kentucky University, Transylvania University,
University of Kentucky, University of Louisville,
and Western Kentucky University.
Editorial and Sales Offices: Lexington, Kentucky 40508-4008

Library of Congress Cataloging-in-Publication Data
Home voices : a sampler of southern writing / Mark Lucas, editor.
    p.   cm. — (New books for new readers)
    ISBN 0-8131-0906-X
    1. Southern States—Literary collections.   2. American literature
—Southern States.   3. Readers for new literates.   I. Lucas, Mark,
1953-   . II. Series.
PS551.H63   1991
810.8'0975'0904—dc20   90-24521

This book is printed on acid-free paper meeting
the requirements of the American National Standard
for Permanence of Paper for Printed Library Materials. ∞

Contents

To my 2nd Best Buddy Malcolm who carries the name of my dear Daddy. I am so very proud of the man you are becoming and hope I live long enough to witness your bright future.

With Love & Pride

Paw Paw

12/25/19

For Christmas

Malcolm, I have read all of these stories and enjoyed them. They are very good and written by excellent authors. I know you will enjoy them too.

Paw Paw

- 2 -

Foreword

The New Books for New Readers project was made possible through funding from the National Endowment for the Humanities, the Kentucky Humanities Council, *The Kentucky Post,* and Financial Women International. The co-sponsorship and continuing assistance of the Kentucky Department for Libraries and Archives and the Kentucky Literacy Commission have been essential to our undertaking. We are also grateful for the advice and support provided to us by the University Press of Kentucky. All these agencies share our commitment to the important role that reading books should play in the lives of the people of our state, and their belief in this project has made it possible.

The Kentucky Humanities Council sees the campaign for adult literacy as closely linked to our own mission, to make the rich heritage of the humanities accessible to all Kentuckians. Because the printed word is a vital source of this heritage, we believe that books about our state's history and culture written for adult literacy students can help us bring the humanities to Kentucky citizens who might not otherwise have the opportunity to participate in our programs. We offer these books in the hope that, in content and by example, they will be of value to adult new readers.

Virginia G. Smith, Executive Director
Kentucky Humanities Council

Preface

Home Voices is a gathering of six works by Southern writers. The stories are simple enough in words and sentences for people fairly new to reading, yet rich enough in meaning for people not at all new to life. They are arranged in order of difficulty, the easier ones first.

The South has produced much of the greatest American literature of this century. It also has long had the worst literacy rate in the country. But many of the South's nonreaders, with the help of literacy projects springing up all over, are learning to read now. Wouldn't these new readers like a taste of the famous storytelling art of their region? Such readers will recognize not only the words but also the voices in these stories. They are home voices.

Many of the adult new readers I have met have big dreams. They know that the same skill that enables them to read warning labels can take them through the King James Bible some day. This book is for them.

The Kentucky organization of Financial Women International arranged funding for the anthology through their local financial institutions. The vision and helping spirit of FWI are deeply appreciated.

Very special thanks go also to Gail Howe and my Danville team of readers and tutors who donated so much time and good sense: Rodney Hampton, Ann Harney, Paula Ramsay, Debbie LeFevers, Rodney Rawlings, Judy Schaefer, Philip Waddell, and Roger Trent. They were the teachers and I was the student. Warm thanks go to Phyllis MacAdam, editor's editor. Without her patience, energy, and wide knowledge, this book would not have happened. And thanks to all the people at the Kentucky Humanities Council; to readers at the Henry County and Harlan County literacy programs; to Pat Barkley and Operation Read in Lexington; to James Still and David Bottoms; to James M. Gifford of the Jesse Stuart Foundation; to the Boyle County

Public Library; and to other advisors and supporters along the way: Jim Wayne Miller, Eloise Warming, Janice Murphy, George Ella Lyon, Patricia Carey, Annabel Girard—and, as always, my own home voices, Sarah, Will, and Mandy Lucas.

"I'm lonely—
I'll make me a world."

*This poem tells an old story in new words, the words
of an inspired black preacher.*

The Creation

James Weldon Johnson

And God stepped out on space,
And He looked around and said,
*"I'm lonely—
I'll make me a world."*

And far as the eye of God could see
Darkness covered everything,
Blacker than a hundred midnights
Down in a cypress swamp.

Then God smiled,
And the light broke,
And the darkness rolled up on one side,
And the light stood shining on the other,
And God said, *"That's good!"*

Then God reached out and took the light in His
    hands,
And God rolled the light around in His hands,
Until He made the sun;
And He set that sun a-blazing in the heavens.

1

And the light that was left from making the sun
God gathered up in a shining ball
And flung against the darkness,
Spangling the night with the moon and stars.
Then down between
The darkness and the light
He hurled the world;
And God said, *"That's good!"*

Then God himself stepped down—
And the sun was on His right hand,
And the moon was on His left;
The stars were clustered about His head,
And the earth was under His feet.
And God walked, and where He trod
His footsteps hollowed the valleys out
And bulged the mountains up.

Then He stopped and looked and saw
That the earth was hot and barren.
So God stepped over to the edge of the world
And He spat out the seven seas;
He batted His eyes, and the lightnings flashed;
He clapped His hands, and the thunders rolled;
And the waters above the earth came down,
The cooling waters came down.

Then the green grass sprouted,
And the little red flowers blossomed,
The pine-tree pointed his finger to the sky,

And the oak spread out his arms;
The lakes cuddled down in the hollows of the ground,
And the rivers ran down to the sea;
And God smiled again,
And the rainbow appeared,
And curled itself around His shoulder.

Then God raised His arm and He waved His hand
Over the sea and over the land,
And He said, *"Bring forth! Bring forth!"*
And quicker than God could drop His hand,
Fishes and fowls
And beasts and birds
Swam the rivers and the seas,
Roamed the forests and the woods,
And split the air with their wings,
And God said, *"That's good!"*

Then God walked around
And God looked around
On all that He had made.
He looked at His sun,
And He looked at His moon,
And He looked at His little stars;
He looked on His world
With all its living things,
And God said, *"I'm lonely still."*

Then God sat down
On the side of a hill where He could think;

By a deep, wide river He sat down;
With His head in His hands,
God thought and thought,
Till He thought, *"I'll make me a man!"*

Up from the bed of the river
God scooped the clay;
And by the bank of the river
He kneeled Him down;
And there the great God Almighty,
Who lit the sun and fixed it in the sky,
Who flung the stars to the most far corner of the
     night,
Who rounded the earth in the middle of His hand—
This Great God,
Like a mammy bending over her baby,
Kneeled down in the dust
Toiling over a lump of clay
Till He shaped it in His own image;
Then into it He blew the breath of life,
And man became a living soul.
Amen. Amen.

"A snake is an enemy to me."

A father stands to learn a thing or two from his son in this story about love and hate.

Love
Jesse Stuart

Yesterday when the bright sun blazed down on the wilted corn my father and I walked around the edge of the new ground to plan a fence. The cows kept coming through the chestnut oaks on the cliff and running over the young corn. They bit off the tips of the corn and trampled down the stubble.

My father walked in the cornbalk. Bob, our Collie, walked in front of my father. We heard a ground squirrel whistle down over the bluff among the dead treetops at the clearing's edge. "Whoop, take him Bob," said my father. He lifted up a young stalk of corn, with wilted dried roots, where the ground squirrel had dug it up for the sweet grain of corn left on its tender roots. This has been a dry spring and the corn has kept well in the earth where the grain has sprouted. The ground squirrels love this corn. They dig up rows of it and eat the sweet grains. The young corn stalks are killed and we have to replant the corn.

I can see my father kept sicking Bob after the

ground squirrel. He jumped over the corn rows. He started to run toward the ground squirrel. I, too, started running toward the clearing's edge where Bob was jumping and barking. The dust flew in tiny swirls behind our feet. There was a cloud of dust behind us.

"It's a big bull blacksnake," said my father. "Kill him Bob! Kill him Bob!"

Bob was jumping and snapping at the snake so as to make it strike and throw itself off guard. Bob has killed twenty-eight copperheads this spring. He knows how to kill a snake. He doesn't rush to do it. He takes his time and does the job well.

"Let's don't kill the snake," I said. "A blacksnake is a harmless snake. It kills poison snakes. It kills the copperhead. It catches more mice from the fields than a cat."

I could see the snake didn't want to fight the dog. The snake wanted to get away. Bob wouldn't let it. I wondered why it was crawling toward a heap of black loamy earth at the bench of the hill. I wondered why it had come from the chestnut oak sprouts and the matted greenbriars on the cliff. I looked as the snake lifted its pretty head in response to one of Bob's jumps. "It's not a bull blacksnake," I said. "It's a she-snake. Look at the white on her throat."

6

"A snake is an enemy to me," my father snapped. "I hate a snake. Kill it Bob. Go on in there and get that snake and quit playing with it!"

Bob obeyed my father. I hated to see him take this snake by the throat. She was so beautifully poised in the sunlight. Bob grabbed the white patch on her throat. He cracked her long body like an ox whip in the wind. He cracked it against the wind only. The blood spurted from her fine-curved throat. Something hit against my legs like pellets. Bob threw the snake down. I looked to see what had struck my legs. It was snake eggs. Bob had slung them from her body. She was going to the sand heap to lay her eggs, where the sun is the setting-hen that warms them and hatches them.

Bob grabbed her body there on the earth where the red blood was running down on the gray-piled loam. Her body was still writhing in pain. She acted like a green-weed held over a new-ground fire. Bob slung her viciously many times. He cracked her limp body against the wind. She was now limber as a shoestring in the wind. Bob threw her riddled body back on the sand. She quivered like a leaf in a lazy wind, then her riddled body lay perfectly still. The blood colored the loamy earth around the snake.

"Look at the eggs, won't you?" said my father. We counted thirty-seven eggs. I picked an egg up and held it in my hand. Only a minute ago there was life in it. It was an immature seed. It would not hatch. Mother sun could not incubate it on the warm earth. The egg I held in my hand was almost the size of a quail's egg. The shell on it was thin and tough and the egg appeared under the surface to be a watery egg.

"Well, Bob, I guess you see now why this snake couldn't fight," I said. "It is life. Weaker devour the stronger even among human beings. Dog kills snake. Snake kills birds. Birds kill the butterflies. Man conquers all. Man, too, kills for sport."

Bob was panting. He walked ahead of us back to the house. His tongue was out of his mouth. He was tired. He was hot under his shaggy coat of hair. His tongue nearly touched the dry dirt and white flecks of foam dripped from it. We walked toward the house. Neither my father nor I spoke. I still thought about the dead snake. The sun was going down over the chestnut ridge. A lark was singing. It was late for a lark to sing. The red evening clouds floated above the pine trees on our pasture hill. My father stood beside the path. His black hair was moved by the wind. His face was red in the blue wind of day. His eyes looked toward the sinking sun.

"And my father hates a snake," I thought.

I thought about the agony women know of giving

8

birth. I thought about how they will fight to save their children. Then, I thought of the snake. I thought it was silly for me to think such thoughts.

This morning my father and I got up with the chickens. He says one has to get up with the chickens to do a day's work. We got the posthole digger, ax, spud, measuring pole and the mattock. We started for the clearing's edge. Bob didn't go along.

The dew was on the corn. My father walked behind with the posthole digger across his shoulder. I walked in front. The wind was blowing. It was a good morning wind to breathe and a wind that makes one feel like he can get under the edge of a hill and heave the whole hill upside down.

I walked out the corn row where we had come yesterday afternoon. I looked in front of me. I saw something. I saw it moved. It was moving like a huge black rope winds around a windlass. "Steady," I says to my father. "Here is the bull blacksnake." He took one step up beside me and stood. His eyes grew wide apart.

"What do you know about this," he said.

"You have seen the bull blacksnake now," I said. "Take a good look at him! He is lying beside his dead mate. He has come to her. He, perhaps, was on her trail yesterday."

9

The male snake had trailed her to her doom. He had come in the night, under the roof of stars, as the moon shed rays of light on the quivering clouds of green. He had found his lover dead. He was coiled beside her, and she was dead.

The bull blacksnake lifted his head and followed us as we walked around the dead snake. He would have fought us to his death. He would have fought Bob to his death. "Take a stick," said my father, "and throw him over the hill so Bob won't find him. Did you ever see anything to beat that? I've heard they'd do that. But this is my first time to see it." I took a stick and threw him over the bank into the dewy sprouts on the cliff.

"A big house draws kinfolks like a horse draws nitflies."

Mother has a problem. There were already too many mouths to feed. Now two cousins and a great-uncle have come to stay.

[Fire on Little Carr Creek]

From the novel River of Earth *by James Still*

The mines on Little Carr closed in March. Winter had been mild, the snows scant and frost-thin upon the ground. Robins stayed the season through, and sapsuckers came early to drill the black birch beside our house. Though Father had worked in the mines, we did not live in the camps. He owned the scrap of land our house stood upon, a garden patch, and the black birch that was the only tree on all the barren slope above Blackjack. There were three of us children running barefoot over the puncheon floors, and since the year's beginning Mother carried a fourth balanced on one hip as she worked over the rusty stove in the shedroom. There were eight in the family to cook for. Two of Father's cousins, Harl and Tibb Logan, came with the closing of the mines and did not go away.

"It's all we can do to keep bread in the children's mouths," Mother told Father. "Even if they are your blood kin, we can't feed them much longer." Mother knew the strings of shucky beans dried in the fall would not last until a new garden could be raised. A half-dozen soup bones and some meat rinds were left in the smokehouse; skippers had got into a pork shoulder during the unnaturally warm December, and it had to be thrown away. Mother ate just enough for the baby, picking at her food and chewing it in little bites. Father ate sparingly, cleaning his plate of every crumb. His face was almost as thin as Mother's. Harl and Tibb fed well, and grumblingly, upon beans and corn pone. They kicked each other under the table, carrying on a secret joke from day to day, and grimacing at us as they ate. We were pained, and felt foolish because we could not join in their laughter. "You'll have to ask them to go," Mother told Father. "These lazy louts are taking food out of the baby's mouth. What we have won't last forever." Father did not speak for a long time; then he said simply: "I can't turn my kin out." He would say no more.

Mother began to feed us between meals, putting less on the table. They would chuckle without saying anything. Sometimes one of them would make a clucking noise in his throat, but none of us laughed, not even Euly. We would look at Father, his chin drooped over his shirt collar, his eyes lowered. And Fletch's face would be as grave as Father's. Only the baby's face would become bird-eyed and bright.

When Uncle Samp, Father's great-uncle, came for a couple of days and stayed on after the week-end was over, Mother spoke sternly to Father. Father became angry and stamped his foot on the floor. "As long as we've got a crust, it'll never be said I turned my folks from my door," he said. We children were frightened. We had never seen Father storm like this, or heard him raise his voice at Mother. Father was so angry he took his rifle-gun and went off into the woods for the day, bringing in four squirrels for supper. He had barked them, firing at the tree trunk beside the animals' heads, and bringing them down without a wound.

Uncle Samp was a large man. His skin was soft and white, with small pink veins webbing his cheeks and nose. There were no powder burns on his face and hands, and no coal dust ground into the heavy wrinkles of his neck. He had a thin gray mustache, over a hand-span in length, wrapped like a loose cord around his ears. He vowed it had not been trimmed in thirty years. It put a spell on us all, Father's cousins included. We looked at the mustache and felt an itching uneasiness. That night at the table Harl and Tibb ate squirrels' breasts and laughed, winking at each other as they brushed up brown gravy on pieces of corn pone. Uncle Samp told us what this good eating put him in mind of, and he bellowed, his laughter coming deep out of him. The rio lamp trembled on the table. We laughed, watching his face redden with every gust, watching the mustache hang miraculously over his ears. Suddenly my brother Fletch began to cry over his plate. His shins had been kicked under the table. Mother's face paled, her eyes becoming hard and dark. She gave the baby to Father and took Fletch into another room. We ate quietly during the rest of the meal, Father looking sternly down the table.

After supper Mother and Father took a lamp and went out to the smokehouse. We followed, finding them bent over the meat box. Father dug into the salt with a plow blade, Mother holding the light above him. He uncovered three curled rinds of pork. We stayed in the smokehouse a long time, feeling contented and together. The room was large, and we jumped around like savages and swung head-down from the rafters.

Father crawled around on his hands and knees with the baby on his back. Mother sat on a sack of black walnuts and watched us. "Hit's the first time we've been alone in two months," she said. "If we lived in here, there wouldn't be room for anybody else. And it would be healthier than that leaky shack we stay in." Father kept crawling with the baby, kicking up his feet like a spoiled nag. Fletch hurt his leg again. He gritted his teeth and showed us the purple spot where he had been kicked. Father rubbed the bruise and made it feel better. "Their hearts are black as Satan," Mother said. "I'd rather live in this smokehouse than stay down there with them. A big house draws kinfolks like a horse draws nitflies."

It was late when we went to the house. The sky was overcast and starless. During the night, rain came suddenly, draining through the rotten shingles. Father got up in the dark and pushed the beds about. He bumped against a footboard and wakened me. I heard Uncle Samp snoring in the next room; and low and indistinct through the sound of water on the roof came the quiver of laughter. Harl and Tibb were awake in the next room. They were mightily tickled about something. They laughed in long, choking spasms. The sound came to me as though afar off, and I reckon they had their heads under the covers so as not to waken Uncle Samp. I listened and wondered how it was possible to laugh with all the dark and rain.

Morning was bright and rain-fresh. The sharp sunlight fell slantwise upon the worn limestone earth of the hills, and our house squatted weathered and dark on the bald slope. Yellow-bellied sapsuckers drilled their oblong holes in the black birch by the house, now leafing from tight-curled buds. Fletch and I had climbed into the tree before breakfast, and when Mother called us in we were hungry for our boiled wheat.

We were alone at the table, Harl and Tibb having left at daylight for Blackjack. They had left without their breakfast, and this haste seemed strange to Mother. "This is the first meal they've missed," she said.

Uncle Samp slept on in the next room, his head buried under a quilt to keep the light out of his face. Mother fed the baby at her breast, standing by Father at the table. We ate our wheat without sugar, and when we had finished, Mother said to Father: "We have enough bran for three more pans of bread. If the children eat it by themselves, it might last a week. It won't last us all more than three meals. Your kin will have to go today."

Father put his spoon down with a clatter. "My folks eat when we eat," he said, "and as long as we eat." The corners of his mouth were drawn tight into his face. His eyes burned, but there was no anger in them. "I'll get some meal at the store," he said.

Mother leaned against the wall, clutching the baby. Her voice was like ice. "They won't let you have it on credit. You've tried before. We've got to live small. We've got to start over again, hand to mouth, the way we began." She laid her hand upon the air, marking the words with nervous fingers. "We've got to tie ourselves up in such a knot nobody else can get in." Father got his hat and stalked to the door. "We've got to do hit today," she called. But Father was gone, out of the house and over the hill toward Blackjack.

Mother put the baby in the empty wood box while she washed dishes. Euly helped her, clearing the table and setting out a bowl of boiled wheat for Uncle Samp. I went outside with Fletch, and we were driving the sapsuckers from the birch when Uncle Samp shouted in the house. His voice crashed through the wall, pouring between the seamy timbers in raw blasts of anger. Fletch was up in the tree, near the tiptop, so I ran ahead of him into the shedroom. Mother stood in the middle of the floor listening. Baby Green jumped up and down in the wood box. Euly ran behind the stove.

I ran into the room where Uncle Samp was and saw him stride from the looking glass to the bed. His mouth was slack. A low growl flowed out of him. He stopped when he saw me, drawing himself up in his wrath. Then I saw his face, and I was frightened. I was suddenly paralyzed with fear. His face was fiery, the red web of veins straining in his flesh, and his mustache, which had been cut off within an inch of his lips, sticking out like two small gray horns. He rushed upon me, caught me up in his arms, and flung me against the wall. I fell upon the floor, breathless, not uttering a sound. Mother was beside me in a moment, her hands weak and palsied as she lifted me.

I was only frightened, and not hurt. Mother cried a little, making a dry sniffling sound through her nose; then she got up and walked outside and around the house. Uncle Samp was not in sight. She came back and gave Fletch the key to the smokehouse. "We're going to move up there," she said. "Go unlock the door." I helped Euly carry the baby out in the wood box. We set him on the shady side of the woodpile. We began to move the furniture, putting the smaller things in the smokehouse, but leaving the chairs, beds, and tables on the ground halfway between. The stove was heaviest of all, and still hot. The rusty legs broke off on one side, and the other two bent under it. We managed to slide it into the yard. Mother carried the clock and the rio lamp to the smokehouse. The clock rattled with four pennies Fletch kept inside it.

After everything had been taken out we waited in the backyard while Mother went around the house again, looking off the hill. Uncle Samp was nowhere in sight, and neither Harl nor Tibb could be seen.

Then she went inside alone. She stayed a long time.
We could hear her moving across the floor. When
she came out and closed the door there was a haze of
smoke behind her, blue and smelling of burnt wood.

In a moment we saw the flames through the back
window. The rooms were lighted up, and fire ran up
the walls, eating into the old timbers. It climbed to
the ceiling, burst through the roof, and ate the rotten
shingles like leaves. Fletch and I watched the
sapsuckers fly in noisy haste from the black birch,
and he began to cry hoarsely as the young leaves
wilted and hung limp from scorched twigs. The birch
trunk steamed in the heat.

When the flames were highest, leaping through the
charred rafters, a gun fired repeatedly in the valley.
Someone there had noticed the smoke and was
arousing the folks along Little Carr Creek. When
they arrived, the walls had fallen in, and Mother stood
among the scattered furnishings, her face calm and
triumphant.

"But boy howdy, I was alive! Thank you, Jesus."

*It is the year 1906 in the little town of Cold Sassy,
Georgia. A boy and his dog wander out to the
railroad bridge on a lazy afternoon. It becomes a
day they will remember.*

[The Train Trestle]

From the novel Cold Sassy Tree
by Olive Ann Burns

Following behind me, T.R. crouched low and took
a few careful steps onto the trestle. Then, whining,
he turned and crawled back to solid ground, tail
between his legs, and commenced begging me to
come back, too.

When the dog saw I was laughing at him, he wet
on the rail, scratched with his back paws in the dirt,
and dashed off, trying to get me to play chase. After
that didn't work, he bounded down the brambly path
to the creek below, where we had just come from, and
splashed over to the other side, trying to show me a
better way to get there. Standing in the shallow
water, T.R. barked and bragged his white-tipped tail
like he'd done something to get praised for.

"Old yeller belly!" I called down to him,
laughing. My voice echoed spooky between trestle

and water and gorge. I sure wished Pink Predmore and them were up here with me.

I put one bare foot on the rail. It was hot but not enough to burn, so I walked on it a piece, arms spread-eagle, balancing with my fishing pole like a tightrope-walker at the circus. I remember wondering if any birds ever walked through the sky up there instead of flying over the gorge. I soon passed the sand barrel that was bolted onto the trestle beside the tracks. People have been known to jump into a trestle barrel if a train comes at the wrong time and they get trapped.

Two thirds of the way across, I stepped off the rail onto a crosstie and sat down, elbows on knees, to look around. I thought about putting a penny on the tracks for the train to flatten, then decided not to. The penny would fall in the creek. So I just sat there, looking way off, and tried to think who lived in that little white farmhouse with green shutters down in the valley. From up here the house looked like a fresh-painted toy. I wondered why nobody ever painted their houses out in Banks County, where Grandpa Tweedy lived. He didn't know what a can of paint looked like.

Enjoying the breeze, I stretched out, face down, to look through the crossties at the water below. Leaves floated on the creek like tiny boats. And here came a long stick, a wake trailing behind it. When the stick turned against the current to swim toward the bank, I saw it was a water moccasin and threw a cinder at it. I missed the snake, but my next cinder hit the white spot on old T.R.'s rump. He barked at me till he got distracted by a big terrapin crawling on the creek bank. . . .

All of a sudden I saw T.R. raise his head to listen. Then he dashed up the path on the far side of the creek, barking all the way, and went to jumping around at the edge of the trestle. He like to had a fit for me to come on. Shoot, you'd think he heard the train or something. Wasn't near time for the train. I didn't hear anything myself except that dern dog barking.

But just to make sure, I moved my head over to the rail and put an ear against it, lazy-like, and—I could hear the clickety-clack! The train was coming! Well, I could make it easy. But as I scrambled to my feet, the fishing pole got wedged somehow between the rail and crosstie. Couldn't leave it that way. Might derail the train. By the time I got it loose, the clickety-clacks were plain as day and getting louder, *louder,* LOUDER!

I stumbled and fell. Jerking myself up, I saw I couldn't possibly get off the trestle before the train moved onto it. Like a fox who runs into a hound, I turned and sprinted the other way. From somewhere, as in a dream, I heard a scream and looked back just as the big smoking engine roared around a bend.

I knew the engineer saw me. His whistle was going *whoo-whoo-whoo* in quick fast blasts. The trestle shook like a leaf as the train hit it.

I thought to aim for the sand barrel.

God A'mighty help me, I wasn't go'n make it! *Jump!* No, too far, creek too low. . . . Whistle screeching in my ears. . . . Train heat almost at my heels. . . . *Whoo-whoo-whoo!*

At that moment I thought FALL!

Like a doll pushed from behind, I fell face down between the rails and lay flat and thin as I could, head low between crossties, arms stretched overhead. As I was swallowed up in fire and thunder, I hugged my arms tight against my ears.

The engine's roar pierced my eardrums anyway, making awful pain. I was so scared I could hardly breathe, and there was a strong smell of heated creosote. Hot cinders spit on me from the firebox. Yet even as the boxcars clacked, knocked, strained, ground, and groaned overhead, it came to me that I wasn't dead. If there wasn't a dragging brake beam to rip me down the back, I was go'n make it!

Boy howdy, I did some fancy praying. All it amounted to was "God save me! Please God save me!" And then it was "Thank you, Lord, thank you, God, thank you, sir. . . ." I guess what made it seem fancy was the strange peaceful feeling I got, as if the Lord had said, "Well done, thou good and faithful servant," or something like that. I wasn't dead! Boy howdy, boy howdy, boy howdy! I was buried alive in noise, and the heat and cinders stung my neck and legs and the bottoms of my feet. Still and all, that was what kept reminding me I wasn't dead.

I found myself counting boxcars, by the sound of them, which was a long sight different in this position, with my eyes shut tight against the dust and cinders, from being in Cold Sassy waiting for the train to get by so I could cross from South Main to North Main. The train had to end. Trains always do. It seemed like this one never would, but brakes were screeching and the clickety-clacks on the rails were slowing, so I knew the engineer was trying to stop.

I felt blistered from the heat. My straw hat was gone. My arms were so tight against my head that my ears felt numb, yet it wouldn't have hurt more if knives were being jabbed into my eardrums.

But boy howdy, I was alive! Thank you, Jesus.

All of a sudden I felt sunshine overhead. Opening my eyes and raising my head, I saw the red caboose getting smaller and smaller as it neared the end of the trestle. The shaking of the trestle stopped. All sounds were muted, as if I had a wad of thick cotton in both ears or was shut up in a padded closet. I felt limp and dizzy. And as knowledge of what could of happened hit me, I started shaking and crying.

I heard T.R. barking from what seemed like far off, but all of a sudden his tongue was on my face! By gosh, he had run out over that trestle he was so scared of! I grabbed and hugged him, crying, "Good ole dog, good ole T.R.!"

"Nothing is like it used to be, lady. . . . The world is almost rotten."

A drifter comes walking down the road to Lucynell Crater's farm. Mrs. Crater sees him as someone who can fix the place up. He has his eyes on the car in the shed.

The Life You Save May Be Your Own
Flannery O'Connor

The old woman and her daughter were sitting on their porch when Mr. Shiftlet came up their road for the first time. The old woman slid to the edge of her chair and leaned forward, shading her eyes from the piercing sunset with her hand. The daughter could not see far in front of her and continued to play with her fingers. Although the old woman lived in this desolate spot with only her daughter and she had never seen Mr. Shiftlet before, she could tell, even from a distance, that he was a tramp and no one to be afraid of. His left coat sleeve was folded up to show there was only half an arm in it and his gaunt figure listed slightly to the side as if the breeze were pushing him. He had on a black town suit and a brown felt hat that was turned up in the front and down in the back and he carried a tin tool box by a handle. He came on, at an amble, up her road, his face turned toward the sun which appeared to be balancing itself on the peak of a small mountain.

The old woman didn't change her position until he was almost into her yard; then she rose with one hand fisted on her hip. The daughter, a large girl in a short blue organdy dress, saw him all at once and jumped up and began to stamp and point and make excited speechless sounds.

Mr. Shiftlet stopped just inside the yard and set his box on the ground and tipped his hat at her as if she were not in the least afflicted; then he turned toward the old woman and swung the hat all the way off. He had long black hair that hung flat from a part in the middle to beyond the tips of his ears on either side. His face descended in forehead for more than half its length and ended suddenly with his features just balanced over a jutting steeltrap jaw. He seemed to be a young man but he had a look of composed dissatisfaction as if he understood life thoroughly.

"Good evening," the old woman said. She was about the size of a cedar fence post and she had a man's gray hat pulled down low over her head.

The tramp stood looking at her and didn't answer. He turned his back and faced the sunset. He swung both his whole and his short arm up slowly so that they indicated an expanse of sky and his figure formed a crooked cross. The old woman watched him with her arms folded across her chest as if she were the owner of the sun, and the daughter watched, her head thrust forward and her fat helpless hands hanging at the wrists. She had long pink-gold hair and eyes as blue as a peacock's neck.

He held the pose for almost fifty seconds and then he picked up his box and came on to the porch and dropped down on the bottom step. "Lady," he said in a firm nasal voice, "I'd give a fortune to live where I could see me a sun do that every evening."

"Does it every evening," the old woman said and sat back down. The daughter sat down too and watched him with a cautious sly look as if he were a bird that had come up very close. He leaned to one side, rooting in his pants pocket, and in a second he brought out a package of chewing gum and offered her a piece. She took it and unpeeled it and began to chew without taking her eyes off him. He offered the old woman a piece but she only raised her upper lip to indicate she had no teeth.

Mr. Shiftlet's pale sharp glance had already passed over everything in the yard—the pump near the corner of the house and the big fig tree that three or four chickens were preparing to roost in—and had moved to a shed where he saw the square rusted back of an automobile. "You ladies drive?" he asked.

"That car ain't run in fifteen year," the old woman said. "The day my husband died, it quit running."

"Nothing is like it used to be, lady," he said. "The world is almost rotten."

"That's right," the old woman said. "You from around here?"

"Name Tom T. Shiftlet," he murmured, looking at the tires.

"I'm pleased to meet you," the old woman said. "Name Lucynell Crater and daughter Lucynell Crater. What you doing around here, Mr. Shiftlet?"

He judged the car to be about a 1928 or '29 Ford. "Lady," he said, and turned and gave her his full attention, "lemme tell you something. There's one of these doctors in Atlanta that's taken a knife and cut the human heart—the human heart," he repeated, leaning forward, "out of a man's chest and held it in his hand," and he held his hand out, palm up, as if it were slightly weighted with the human heart, "and studied it like it was a day-old chicken, and lady," he said, allowing a long significant pause in which his head slid forward and his clay-colored eyes brightened, "he don't know no more about it than you or me."

"That's right," the old woman said.

"Why, if he was to take that knife and cut into every corner of it, he still wouldn't know no more than you or me. What you want to bet?"

"Nothing," the old woman said wisely. "Where you come from, Mr. Shiftlet?"

He didn't answer. He reached into his pocket and brought out a sack of tobacco and a package of cigarette papers and rolled himself a cigarette, expertly with one hand, and attached it in a hanging position to his upper lip. Then he took a box of wooden matches from his pocket and struck one on his shoe. He held the burning match as if he were studying the mystery of flame while it traveled dangerously toward his skin. The daughter began to make loud noises and to point to his hand and shake her finger at him, but when the flame was just before touching him, he leaned down with his hand cupped over it as if he were going to set fire to his nose and lit the cigarette.

He flipped away the dead match and blew a stream of gray into the evening. A sly look came over his face. "Lady," he said, "nowadays, people'll do anything anyways. I can tell you my name is Tom T.

Shiftlet and I come from Tarwater, Tennessee, but you never have seen me before: how you know I ain't lying? How you know my name ain't Aaron Sparks, lady, and I come from Singleberry, Georgia, or how you know it's not George Speeds and I come from Lucy, Alabama, or how you know I ain't Thompson Bright from Toolafalls, Mississippi?"

"I don't know nothing about you," the old woman muttered, irked.

"Lady," he said, "people don't care how they lie. Maybe the best I can tell you is, I'm a man; but listen lady," he said and paused and made his tone more ominous still, "what is a man?"

The old woman began to gum a seed. "What you carry in that tin box, Mr. Shiftlet?" she asked.

"Tools," he said, put back. "I'm a carpenter."

"Well, if you come out here to work, I'll be able to feed you and give you a place to sleep but I can't pay. I'll tell you that before you begin," she said.

There was no answer at once and no particular expression on his face. He leaned back against the two-by-four that helped support the porch roof. "Lady," he said slowly, "there's some men that some things mean more to them than money." The old woman rocked without comment and the daughter watched the trigger that moved up and down in his neck. He told the old woman then that all most people were interested in was money, but he asked what a man was made for. He asked her if a man was made for money, or what. He asked her what she thought she was made for but she didn't answer, she only sat rocking and wondered if a one-armed man could put a new roof on her garden house. He asked a lot of questions that she didn't answer. He told her that he was twenty-eight years old and had lived a varied life. He had been a gospel singer, a foreman on the railroad, an assistant in an undertaking parlor, and he come over the radio for three months with Uncle Roy and his Red Creek Wranglers. He said he had fought and bled in the Arm Service of his country and visited every foreign land and that everywhere he had seen people that didn't care if they did a thing one way or another. He said he hadn't been raised thataway.

A fat yellow moon appeared in the branches of the fig tree as if it were going to roost there with the chickens. He said that a man had to escape to the country to see the world whole and that he wished he lived in a desolate place like this where he could see the sun go down every evening like God made it to do.

"Are you married or are you single?" the old woman asked.

There was a long silence. "Lady," he asked finally, "where would you find you an innocent woman today? I wouldn't have any of this trash I could just pick up."

The daughter was leaning very far down, hanging her head almost between her knees watching him through a triangular door she had made in her overturned hair; and she suddenly fell in a heap on the floor and began to whimper. Mr. Shiftlet straightened her out and helped her get back in the chair.

"Is she your baby girl?" he asked.

"My only," the old woman said "and she's the sweetest girl in the world. I would give her up for nothing on earth. She's smart too. She can sweep the floor, cook, wash, feed the chickens, and hoe. I wouldn't give her up for a casket of jewels."

"No," he said kindly, "don't ever let any man take her away from you."

"Any man come after her," the old woman said, "'ll have to stay around the place."

Mr. Shiftlet's eye in the darkness was focused on a part of the automobile bumper that glittered in the distance. "Lady," he said, jerking his short arm up as if he could point with it to her house and yard and pump, "there ain't a broken thing on this plantation that I couldn't fix for you, one-arm jackleg or not. I'm a man," he said with a sullen dignity, "even if I ain't a whole one. I got," he said, tapping his knuckles on the floor to emphasize the immensity of what he was going to say, "a moral intelligence!" and his face pierced out of the darkness into a shaft of doorlight and he stared at her as if he were astonished himself at this impossible truth.

The old woman was not impressed with the phrase. "I told you you could hang around and work for food," she said, "if you don't mind sleeping in that car yonder."

"Why listen, lady," he said with a grin of delight, "the monks of old slept in their coffins!"

"They wasn't as advanced as we are," the old woman said.

The next morning he began on the roof of the garden house while Lucynell, the daughter, sat on a rock and watched him work. He had not been around a week before the change he had made in the place was apparent. He had patched the front and back steps, built a new hog pen, restored a fence, and taught Lucynell, who was completely deaf and had never said a word in her life, to say the word "bird." The big rosy-faced girl followed him everywhere, saying "Burrttddt ddbirrrttdt," and clapping her hands. The old woman watched from a distance, secretly pleased. She was ravenous for a son-in-law.

Mr. Shiftlet slept on the hard narrow back seat of the car with his feet out the side window. He had his razor and a can of water on a crate that served him as a bedside table and he put up a piece of mirror against the back glass and kept his coat neatly on a hanger that he hung over one of the windows.

In the evenings he sat on the steps and talked while the old woman and Lucynell rocked violently in their chairs on either side of him. The old woman's three mountains were black against the dark blue sky and were visited off and on by various planets and by the moon after it had left the chickens. Mr. Shiftlet pointed out that the reason he had improved this plantation was because he had taken a personal interest in it. He said he was even going to make the automobile run.

He had raised the hood and studied the mechanism and he said he could tell that the car had been built in the days when cars were really built. You take now, he said, one man puts in one bolt and another man puts in another bolt and another man puts in another bolt so that it's a man for a bolt. That's why you have to pay so much for a car: you're paying all those men. Now if you didn't have to pay but one man, you could get you a cheaper car and one that had had a personal interest taken in it, and it would be a better car. The old woman agreed with him that this was so.

Mr. Shiftlet said that the trouble with the world was that nobody cared, or stopped and took any trouble. He said he never would have been able to teach Lucynell to say a word if he hadn't cared and stopped long enough.

"Teach her to say something else," the old woman said.

"What you want her to say next?" Mr. Shiftlet asked.

The old woman's smile was broad and toothless and suggestive. "Teach her to say 'sugarpie,' " she said.

Mr. Shiftlet already knew what was on her mind.

The next day he began to tinker with the automobile and that evening he told her that if she would buy a fan belt, he would be able to make the car run.

The old woman said she would give him the money. "You see that girl yonder?" she asked, pointing to Lucynell who was sitting on the floor a foot away, watching him, her eyes blue even in the dark. "If it was ever a man wanted to take her away,

I would say, 'No man on earth is going to take that sweet girl of mine away from me!' but if he was to say, 'Lady, I don't want to take her away, I want her right here,' I would say, 'Mister, I don't blame you none. I wouldn't pass up a chance to live in a permanent place and get the sweetest girl in the world myself. You ain't no fool,' I would say."

"How old is she?" Mr. Shiftlet asked casually.

"Fifteen, sixteen," the old woman said. The girl was nearly thirty but because of her innocence it was impossible to guess.

"It would be a good idea to paint it too," Mr. Shiftlet remarked. "You don't want it to rust out."

"We'll see about that later," the old woman said.

The next day he walked into town and returned with the parts he needed and a can of gasoline. Late in the afternoon, terrible noises issued from the shed and the old woman rushed out of the house, thinking Lucynell was somewhere having a fit. Lucynell was sitting on a chicken crate, stamping her feet and screaming, "Burrddttt! bddurrddtttt!" but her fuss was drowned out by the car. With a volley of blasts it emerged from the shed, moving in a fierce and stately way. Mr. Shiftlet was in the driver's seat, sitting very erect. He had an expression of serious modesty on his face as if he had just raised the dead.

That night, rocking on the porch, the old woman began her business, at once. "You want you an innocent woman, don't you?" she asked sympathetically. "You don't want none of this trash."

"No'm, I don't," Mr. Shiftlet said.

"One that can't talk," she continued, "can't sass you back or use foul language. That's the kind for you to have. Right there," and she pointed to Lucynell sitting cross-legged in her chair, holding both feet in her hands.

"That's right," he admitted. "She wouldn't give me any trouble."

"Saturday," the old woman said, "you and her and me can drive into town and get married."

Mr. Shiftlet eased his position on the steps.

"I can't get married right now," he said. "Everything you want to do takes money and I ain't got any."

"What you need with money?" she asked.

"It takes money," he said. "Some people'll do anything anyhow these days, but the way I think, I wouldn't marry no woman that I couldn't take on a trip like she was somebody. I mean take her to a hotel and treat her. I wouldn't marry the Duchesser

Windsor," he said firmly, "unless I could take her to a hotel and giver something good to eat.

"I was raised thataway and there ain't a thing I can do about it. My old mother taught me how to do."

"Lucynell don't even know what a hotel is," the old woman muttered. "Listen here, Mr. Shiftlet," she said, sliding forward in her chair, "you'd be getting a permanent house and a deep well and the most innocent girl in the world. You don't need no money. Lemme tell you something: there ain't any place in the world for a poor disabled friendless drifting man."

The ugly words settled in Mr. Shiftlet's head like a group of buzzards in the top of a tree. He didn't answer at once. He rolled himself a cigarette and lit it and then he said in an even voice, "Lady, a man is divided into two parts, body and spirit."

The old woman clamped her gums together.

"A body and a spirit," he repeated. "The body, lady, is like a house: it don't go anywhere; but the spirit, lady, is like a automobile: always on the move, always . . ."

"Listen, Mr. Shiftlet," she said, "my well never goes dry and my house is always warm in the winter and there's no mortgage on a thing about this place.

You can go to the courthouse and see for yourself. And yonder under that shed is a fine automobile." She laid the bait carefully. "You can have it painted by Saturday. I'll pay for the paint."

In the darkness, Mr. Shiftlet's smile stretched like a weary snake waking up by a fire. After a second he recalled himself and said, "I'm only saying a man's spirit means more to him than anything else. I would have to take my wife off for the weekend without no regards at all for cost. I got to follow where my spirit says to go."

"I'll give you fifteen dollars for a weekend trip," the old woman said in a crabbed voice. "That's the best I can do."

"That wouldn't hardly pay for more than the gas and the hotel," he said. "It wouldn't feed her."

"Seventeen-fifty," the old woman said. "That's all I got so it isn't any use you trying to milk me. You can take a lunch."

Mr. Shiftlet was deeply hurt by the word "milk." He didn't doubt that she had more money sewed up in her mattress but he had already told her he was not interested in her money. "I'll make that do," he said and rose and walked off without treating with her further.

On Saturday the three of them drove into town in

the car that the paint had barely dried on and Mr. Shiftlet and Lucynell were married in the Ordinary's office while the old woman witnessed. As they came out of the courthouse, Mr. Shiftlet began twisting his neck in his collar. He looked morose and bitter as if he had been insulted while someone held him. "That didn't satisfy me none," he said. "That was just something a woman in an office did, nothing but paper work and blood tests. What do they know about my blood? If they was to take my heart and cut it out," he said, "they wouldn't know a thing about me. It didn't satisfy me at all."

"It satisfied the law," the old woman said sharply.

"The law," Mr. Shiftlet said and spit. "It's the law that don't satisfy me."

He had painted the car dark green with a yellow band around it just under the windows. The three of them climbed in the front seat and the old woman said, "Don't Lucynell look pretty? Looks like a baby doll." Lucynell was dressed up in a white dress that her mother had uprooted from a trunk and there was a Panama hat on her head with a bunch of red wooden cherries on the brim. Every now and then her placid expression was changed by a sly isolated little thought like a shoot of green in the desert. "You got a prize!" the old woman said.

Mr. Shiftlet didn't even look at her.

They drove back to the house to let the old woman off and pick up the lunch. When they were ready to leave, she stood staring in the window of the car, with her fingers clenched around the glass. Tears began to seep sideways out of her eyes and run along the dirty creases in her face. "I ain't ever been parted with her for two days before," she said.

Mr. Shiftlet started the motor.

"And I wouldn't let no man have her but you because I seen you would do right. Good-by, Sugarbaby," she said, clutching at the sleeve of the white dress. Lucynell looked straight at her and didn't seem to see her there at all. Mr. Shiftlet eased the car forward so that she had to move her hands.

The early afternoon was clear and open and surrounded by pale blue sky. Although the car would go only thirty miles an hour, Mr. Shiftlet imagined a terrific climb and dip and swerve that went entirely to his head so that he forgot his morning bitterness. He had always wanted an automobile but he had never been able to afford one before. He drove very fast because he wanted to make Mobile by nightfall.

Occasionally he stopped his thoughts long enough to look at Lucynell in the seat beside him. She had eaten the lunch as soon as they were out of the yard and now she was pulling the cherries off the hat one by one and throwing them out the window. He became depressed in spite of the car. He had driven about a hundred miles when he decided that she must be hungry again and at the next small town they came to, he stopped in front of an aluminum-painted eating place called The Hot Spot and took her in and ordered her a plate of ham and grits. The ride had made her sleepy and as soon as she got up on the stool, she rested her head on the counter and shut her eyes. There was no one in The Hot Spot but Mr. Shiftlet and the boy behind the counter, a pale youth with a greasy rag hung over his shoulder. Before he could dish up the food, she was snoring gently.

"Give it to her when she wakes up," Mr. Shiftlet said. "I'll pay for it now."

The boy bent over her and stared at the long pink-gold hair and the half-shut sleeping eyes. Then he looked up and stared at Mr. Shiftlet. "She looks like an angel of Gawd," he murmured.

"Hitchhiker," Mr. Shiftlet explained. "I can't wait. I got to make Tuscaloosa."

The boy bent over again and very carefully touched his finger to a strand of the golden hair and Mr. Shiftlet left.

He was more depressed than ever as he drove on by himself. The late afternoon had grown hot and sultry and the country had flattened out. Deep in the sky a storm was preparing very slowly and without thunder as if it meant to drain every drop of air from the earth before it broke. There were times when Mr. Shiftlet preferred not be be alone. He felt too that a man with a car had a responsibility to others and he kept his eye out for a hitchhiker. Occasionally he saw a sign that warned: "Drive carefully. The life you save may be your own."

The narrow road dropped off on either side into dry fields and here and there a shack or a filling station stood in a clearing. The sun began to set directly in front of the automobile. It was a reddening ball that through his windshield was slightly flat on the bottom and top. He saw a boy in overalls and a gray hat standing on the edge of the road and he slowed the car down and stopped in front of him. The boy didn't have his hand raised to thumb the ride, he was only standing there, but he had a small cardboard suitcase and his hat was set on his head in a way to indicate that he had left somewhere for good. "Son," Mr. Shiftlet said, "I see you want a ride."

The boy didn't say he did or he didn't but he opened the door of the car and got in, and Mr. Shiftlet started driving again. The child held the suitcase on his lap and folded his arms on top of it. He turned his head and looked out the window away from Mr. Shiftlet. Mr. Shiftlet felt oppressed. "Son," he said after a minute, "I got the best old mother in the world so I reckon you only got the second best."

The boy gave him a quick dark glance and then turned his face back out the window.

"It's nothing so sweet," Mr. Shiftlet continued, "as a boy's mother. She taught him his first prayers at her knee, she give him love when no other would, she told him what was right and what wasn't, and she seen that he done the right thing. Son," he said, "I never rued a day in my life like the one I rued when I left that old mother of mine."

The boy shifted in his seat but he didn't look at Mr. Shiftlet. He unfolded his arms and put one hand on the door handle.

"My mother was an angel of Gawd," Mr. Shiftlet said in a very strained voice. "He took her from heaven and giver to me and I left her." His eyes were instantly clouded over with a mist of tears. The car was barely moving.

The boy turned angrily in the seat. "You go to the devil!" he cried. "My old woman is a flea bag and yours is a stinking pole cat!" and with that he flung the door open and jumped out with his suitcase into the ditch.

Mr. Shiftlet was so shocked that for about a

hundred feet he drove along slowly with the door still open. A cloud, the exact color of the boy's hat and shaped like a turnip, had descended over the sun, and another, worse looking, crouched behind the car. Mr. Shiftlet felt that the rottenness of the world was about to engulf him. He raised his arm and let it fall again to his breast. "Oh Lord!" he prayed. "Break forth and wash the slime from this earth!"

The turnip continued slowly to descend. After a few minutes there was a guffawing peal of thunder from behind and fantastic raindrops, like tin-can tops, crashed over the rear of Mr. Shiftlet's car. Very quickly he stepped on the gas and with his stump sticking out the window he raced the galloping shower into Mobile.

"So you have no grandchildren. What a pity in a place like this which two boys would enjoy—sports, fishing, game to shoot at, perhaps the most exciting game of all. . . ."

Mississippi, 1861. Young Bayard Sartoris and his black playmate, Ringo, are in trouble. The two boys have just fired the family musket at a Yankee soldier coming up the road on a horse. Bayard's grandmother has got to think of something fast.

[Civil War]
From the novel The Unvanquished
by William Faulkner

The house didn't seem to get any nearer; it just hung there in front of us, floating and increasing slowly in size, like something in a dream, and I could hear Ringo moaning behind me, and farther back still the shouts and the hoofs. But we reached the house at last; Louvinia was just inside the door, with Father's old hat on her head rag and her mouth open, but we didn't stop. We ran on into the room where Granny was standing beside the righted chair, her hand at her chest.

"We shot him, Granny!" I cried. "We shot the bastud!"

"What?" She looked at me, her face the same

color as her hair almost, her spectacles shining against her hair above her forehead. "Bayard Sartoris, what did you say?"

"We killed him, Granny! At the gate! Only there was the whole army, too, and we never saw them, and now they are coming."

She sat down; she dropped into the chair, hard, her hand at her breast. But her voice was strong as ever:

"What's this? You, Marengo! What have you done?"

"We shot the bastud, Granny!" Ringo said. "We kilt him!"

Then Louvinia was there, too, with her mouth still open, too, and her face like somebody had thrown ashes at her. Only it didn't need her face; we heard the hoofs jerking and sliding in the dirt, and one of them hollering, "Get around to the back there, some of you!" and we looked up and saw them ride past the window—the blue coats and the guns. Then we heard the boots and spurs on the porch.

"Granny!" I said. "Granny!" But it seemed like none of us could move at all, we just had to stand there looking at Granny with her hand at her breast and her face looking like she had died and her voice like she had died too:

"Louvinia! What is this? What are they trying to tell me?" That's how it happened—like when once the musket decided to go off, all that was to occur afterward tried to rush into the sound of it all at once. I could still hear it, my ears were still ringing, so that Granny and Ringo and I all seemed to be talking far away. Then she said, "Quick! Here!" and then Ringo and I were squatting with our knees under our chins, on either side of her against her legs, with the hard points of the chair rockers jammed into our backs and her skirts spread over us like a tent, and the heavy feet coming in and—Louvinia told us afterward—the Yankee sergeant shaking the musket at Granny and saying:

"Come on, grandma! Where are they? We saw them run in here!"

We couldn't see; we just squatted in a kind of faint gray light and that smell of Granny that her clothes and bed and room all had, and Ringo's eyes looking like two plates of chocolate pudding and maybe both of us thinking how Granny had never whipped us for anything in our lives except lying, and that even when it wasn't even a told lie, but just keeping quiet, how she would whip us first and then make us kneel down and kneel down with us herself to ask the Lord to forgive us.

"You are mistaken," she said. "There are no

children in this house nor on this place. There is no one here at all except my servant and myself and the people in the quarters."

"You mean you deny ever having seen this gun before?"

"I do." It was that quiet; she didn't move at all, sitting bolt upright and right on the edge of the chair, to keep her skirts spread over us. "If you doubt me, you may search the house."

"Don't you worry about that; I'm going to. . . . Send some of the boys upstairs," he said. "If you find any locked doors, you know what to do. And tell them fellows out back to comb the barn and the cabins too."

"You won't find any locked doors," Granny said. "At least, let me ask you——"

"Don't you ask anything, grandma. You set still. Better for you if you had done a little asking before you sent them little devils out with this gun."

"Was there——" We could hear her voice die away and then speak again, like she was behind it with a switch, making it talk. "Is he—it—the one who ——"

"Dead? Hell, yes! Broke his back and we had to shoot him!"

"Had to—you had—shoot———" I didn't know horrified astonishment either, but Ringo and Granny and I were all three it.

"Yes, by God! Had to shoot him! The best horse in the whole army! The whole regiment betting on him for next Sunday———" He said some more, but we were not listening. We were not breathing either, glaring at each other in the gray gloom, and I was almost shouting, too, until Granny said it:

"Didn't—they didn't——— Oh, thank God! Thank God!"

"We didn't———" Ringo said.

"Hush!" I said. Because we didn't have to say it, it was like we had had to hold our breaths for a long time without knowing it, and that now we could let go and breathe again. Maybe that was why we never heard the other man, when he came in, at all; it was Louvinia that saw that, too—a colonel, with a bright short beard and hard bright gray eyes, who looked at Granny sitting in the chair with her hand at her breast, and took off his hat. Only he was talking to the sergeant.

"What's this?" he said. "What's going on here, Harrison?"

"This is where they run to," the sergeant said. "I'm searching the house."

"Ah," the colonel said. He didn't sound mad at all. He just sounded cold and short and pleasant. "By whose authority?"

"Well, somebody here fired on United States troops. I guess this is authority enough." We could just hear the sound; it was Louvinia that told us how he shook the musket and banged the butt on the floor.

"And killed one horse," the colonel said.

"It was a United States horse. I heard the general say myself that if he had enough horses, he wouldn't always care whether there was anybody to ride them or not. And so here we are, riding peaceful along the road, not bothering nobody yet, and these two little devils—— The best horse in the army; the whole regiment betting——"

"Ah," the colonel said. "I see. Well? Have you found them?"

"We ain't yet. But these rebels are like rats when it comes to hiding. She says that there ain't even any children here."

"Ah," said the colonel. And Louvinia said how he looked at Granny now for the first time. She said how she could see his eyes going from Granny's face down to where her skirt was spread, and looking at her skirt for a whole minute and then going back to her face. And that Granny gave him look for look while she lied. "Do I understand, madam, that there are no children in or about this house?"

"There are none, sir," Granny said.

Louvinia said he looked back at the sergeant. "There are no children here, sergeant. Evidently the shot came from somewhere else. You may call the men in and mount them."

"But, colonel, we saw them two kids run in here! All of us saw them!"

"Didn't you just hear this lady say there are no children here? Where are your ears, sergeant? Or do you really want the artillery to overtake us, with a creek bottom not five miles away to be got over?"

"Well, sir, you're colonel. But if it was me was colonel——"

"Then, doubtless, I should be Sergeant Harrison. In which case, I think I should be more concerned about getting another horse to protect my wager next Sunday than over a grandchildless old lady"— Louvinia said his eyes just kind of touched Granny now and flicked away—"alone in a house which, in all probability—and for her pleasure and satisfaction, I am ashamed to say, I hope—I shall never see again. Mount your men and get along."

We squatted there, not breathing, and heard them
leave the house; we heard the sergeant calling the
men up from the barn and we heard them ride away.
But we did not move yet, because Granny's body had
not relaxed at all, and so we knew that the colonel
was still there, even before he spoke—the voice short,
brisk, hard, with that something of laughing behind
it: "So you have no grandchildren. What a pity in a
place like this which two boys would enjoy—sports,
fishing, game to shoot at, perhaps the most exciting
game of all, and none the less so for being, possibly,
a little rare this near the house. And with a gun—a
very dependable weapon, I see." Louvinia said how
the sergeant had set the musket in the corner and how
the colonel looked at it now, and now we didn't
breathe. "Though I understand that this weapon does
not belong to you. Which is just as well. Because if
it were your weapon—which it is not—and you had
two grandsons, or say a grandson and a Negro play-
fellow—which you have not—and if this were the
first time—which it is not—someone next time might
be seriously hurt. But what am I doing? Trying your
patience by keeping you in that uncomfortable chair
while I waste my time delivering a homily suitable
only for a lady with grandchildren—or one
grandchild and a Negro companion." Now he was
about to go, too; we could tell it even beneath the
skirt; this time it was Granny herself:

"There is little of refreshment I can offer you, sir. But if a glass of cool milk after your ride——"

Only, for a long time he didn't answer at all; Louvinia said how he just looked at Granny with his hard bright eyes and that hard bright silence full of laughing. "No, no," he said. "I thank you. You are taxing yourself beyond mere politeness and into sheer bravado."

"Louvinia," Granny said, "conduct the gentleman to the dining room and serve him with what we have."

He was out of the room now, because Granny began to tremble now, trembling and trembling, but not relaxing yet; we could hear her panting now. And we breathed, too, now, looking at each other. "We never killed him!" I whispered. "We haven't killed anybody at all!" So it was Granny's body that told us again; only this time I could almost feel him looking at Granny's spread skirt where we crouched while he thanked her for the milk and told her his name and regiment.

"Perhaps it is just as well that you have no grandchildren," he said. "Since, doubtless, you wish to live in peace. I have three boys myself, you see. And I have not even had time to become a grandparent." And now there wasn't any laughing behind his voice, and Louvinia said he was standing there in the door, with the brass bright on his dark blue and his hat in his hand and his bright beard and hair, looking at Granny without the laughing now: "I won't apologise; fools cry out at wind or fire. But permit me to say and hope that you will never have anything worse than this to remember us by." Then he was gone. We heard his spurs in the hall and on the porch, then the horse, dying away, ceasing, and then Granny let go. She went back into the chair with her hand at her breast and her eyes closed and the sweat on her face in big drops; all of a sudden I began to holler, "Louvinia! Louvinia!" But she opened her eyes then and looked at me; they were looking at me when they opened. Then she looked at Ringo for a moment, but she looked back at me, panting.

"Bayard," she said, "what was that word you used?"

"Word?" I said. "When, Granny?" Then I remembered; I didn't look at her, and she lying back in the chair, looking at me and panting.

"Don't repeat it. You cursed. You used obscene language, Bayard."

I didn't look at her. I could see Ringo's feet too. "Ringo did too," I said. She didn't answer, but I could feel her looking at me; I said suddenly: "And you told a lie. You said we were not here."